PETER RABBIT'S CHRISTMAS BOOK

Compiled by Jennie Walters

From the original and authorized stories
BY **BEATRIX POTTER**

™

F. WARNE & Co

BEATRIX POTTER
AND
CHRISTMAS

Christmas in the Potter family household seems to have been a rather quiet affair. Beatrix never wrote about any happy Christmases in the diary she started at the age of fifteen, and her main reference to the festive season comes in 1895, when she was twenty-nine: 'We had not a pleasant Christmas, wet, dark, Bertram sulky.' Bertram, her only brother, was six years younger than Beatrix, and she had a solitary childhood in London, with few friends to play with as she was educated at home by governesses.

Beatrix knew what Christmas should be like, however, as her lovely account of the animals' Christmas party on page 35 shows. She enjoyed celebrations, and later on in life loved to go to the country dances around her Lake District home. Her Peter Rabbit books are full of parties: Mr. Jeremy Fisher has his friends Sir Isaac Newton and Mr. Alderman Ptolemy Tortoise round to dinner, Mrs. Tittlemouse throws a party for her friends after she has finished spring-cleaning and Tom Kitten's mother, Mrs. Tabitha Twitchit, gives a tea party which is disturbed by the naughty kittens.

Christmas is a festival of thanksgiving and a time for starting afresh, as Beatrix Potter also knew. We give presents to our family and friends to tell them how much we appreciate them, and sometimes to make up for things we may have done in the past year. Benjamin and Flopsy Bunny give Mrs. Tittlemouse some rabbit wool to thank her for rescuing their children from Mr. McGregor, and the Two Bad Mice stuff a sixpence into the dolls' Christmas stocking, to say sorry for all the damage they caused in the dolls' house.

Christmas is also a time of magic and wonder. In Beatrix Potter's own words, 'It is in the old story that all the beasts can talk, in the night between Christmas Eve and Christmas Day in the morning (though there are very few folk that can hear them, or know what it is that they say).' If you read her Christmas story, *The Tailor of Gloucester*, you can find out . . . .

CONTENTS

THE TAILOR OF GLOUCESTER

IN the time of swords and periwigs and full-skirted coats with flowered lappets—when gentlemen wore ruffles, and gold-laced waistcoats of paduasoy and taffeta—there lived a tailor in Gloucester.

He sat in the window of a little shop in Westgate Street, cross-legged on a table, from morning till dark.

All day long while the light lasted he sewed and snippeted, piecing out his satin and

pompadour, and lutestring; stuffs had strange names, and were very expensive in the days of the Tailor of Gloucester.

But although he sewed fine silk for his neighbours, he himself was very, very poor—a little old man in spectacles, with a pinched face, old crooked fingers, and a suit of thread-bare clothes.

He cut his coats without waste, according to his embroidered cloth; they were very small ends and snippets that lay about upon the table—"Too narrow breadths for nought—except waistcoats for mice," said the tailor.

One bitter cold day near Christmas-time the tailor began to make a coat—a coat of cherry-coloured corded silk embroidered with pansies and roses, and a cream-coloured satin waistcoat—trimmed with gauze and green worsted chenille—for the Mayor of Gloucester.

The tailor worked and worked, and he talked to himself. He measured the silk, and turned it round and round, and trimmed it into shape with his shears; the table was all littered with cherry-coloured snippets.

"No breadth at all, and cut on the cross; it is no breadth at all; tippets for mice and ribbons for mobs! for mice!" said the Tailor of Gloucester.

When the snow-flakes came down against the small leaded window-panes and shut out the light, the tailor had done his day's work; all the silk and satin lay cut out upon the table.

There were twelve pieces for the coat and four pieces for the waistcoat; and there were pocket flaps and cuffs, and buttons all in order. For the lining of the coat there was fine yellow taffeta; and for the button-holes of the waist-coat, there was cherry-coloured twist. And

everything was ready to sew together in the morning, all measured and sufficient—except that there was wanting just one single skein of cherry-coloured twisted silk.

The tailor came out of his shop at dark, for he did not sleep there at nights; he fastened the window and locked the door, and took away the key. No one lived there at night but little brown mice, and they run in and out without any keys!

For behind the wooden wainscots of all the old houses in Gloucester, there are little mouse staircases and secret trap-doors; and the mice run from house to house through those long narrow passages; they can run all over the town without going into the streets.

But the tailor came out of his shop, and shuffled home through the snow. He lived quite near by in College Court, next the doorway to College Green; and although it was not a big house, the tailor was so poor he only rented the kitchen.

He lived alone with his cat; it was called Simpkin.

Now all day long while the tailor was out at work, Simpkin kept house by himself; and he also was fond of the mice, though he gave them no satin for coats!

"Miaw?" said the cat when the tailor opened the door. "Miaw?"

The tailor replied—"Simpkin, we shall make our fortune, but I am worn to a ravelling. Take this groat (which is our last fourpence) and Simpkin, take a china pipkin; buy a penn'orth of bread, a penn'orth

of milk and a penn'orth of sausages. And oh, Simpkin, with the last penny of our fourpence buy me one penn'orth of cherry-coloured silk. But do not lose the last penny of the fourpence, Simpkin, or I am undone and worn to a thread-paper, for I have NO MORE TWIST."

Then Simpkin again said, "Miaw?" and took the groat and the pipkin, and went out into the dark.

The tailor was very tired and beginning to be ill. He sat down by the hearth and talked to himself about that wonderful coat.

"I shall make my fortune—to be cut bias—the Mayor of Gloucester is to be married on Christmas Day in the morning, and he hath ordered a coat and an embroidered waistcoat—to be lined with yellow taffeta—and the taffeta sufficeth; there is no more left over in snippets than will serve to make tippets for mice—"

Then the tailor started; for suddenly, interrupting him, from the dresser at the other side of the kitchen came a number of little noises—

Tip tap, tip tap, tip tap tip!

"Now what can that be?" said the Tailor of Gloucester, jumping up from his chair. The dresser was covered with crockery and pipkins, willow pattern plates, and tea-cups and mugs.

The tailor crossed the kitchen, and stood quite still beside the dresser, listening, and peering through his spectacles. Again from under a tea-cup, came those funny little noises—

Tip tap, tip tap, tip tap tip!

"This is very peculiar," said the Tailor of Gloucester; and he lifted up the tea-cup which was upside down. Out stepped a little live lady mouse, and made a curtsey to the tailor! Then she hopped away down off the dresser, and under the wainscot.

The tailor sat down again by the fire, warming his poor cold hands, and mumbling to himself—

"The waistcoat is cut out from peach-coloured satin—tambour stitch and rose-buds in beautiful floss silk. Was I wise to entrust my last fourpence to Simpkin? One-and-twenty button-holes of cherry-coloured twist!"

But all at once, from the dresser, there came other little noises:

Tip tap, tip tap, tip tap tip!

"This is passing extraordinary!" said the Tailor of Gloucester, and turned over another tea-cup, which was upside down. Out stepped a little gentleman mouse, and made a bow to the tailor!

And then from all over the dresser came a chorus of little tappings, all sounding together, and answering one another, like watch-beetles in an old worm-eaten window-shutter—

Tip tap, tip tap, tip tap tip!

And out from under tea-cups and from under bowls and basins, stepped other and more little mice who hopped away down off the dresser and under the wainscot.

The tailor sat down, close over the fire, lamenting—"One-and-twenty button-holes of cherry-coloured silk! To be finished by noon of Saturday: and this is Tuesday evening. Was it right to let loose those mice, undoubtedly the property of Simpkin? Alack, I am undone, for I have no more twist!"

The little mice came out again, and listened to the tailor; they took notice of the pattern of that wonderful coat. They whispered to one another about the taffeta lining, and about little mouse tippets.

And then all at once they all ran away together down the passage behind the wainscot, squeaking and calling to one another, as they ran from house to house; and not one mouse was left in the tailor's kitchen when Simpkin came back with the pipkin of milk!

Simpkin opened the door and bounced in, with an angry "G-r-r-miaw!" like a cat that is vexed: for he hated the snow, and there was snow in his ears, and snow in his collar at the back of his neck. He put down the loaf and the sausages upon the dresser, and sniffed.

"Simpkin," said the tailor, "where is my twist?"

But Simpkin set down the pipkin of milk upon the dresser, and looked suspiciously at the tea-cups. He wanted his supper of little fat mouse!

"Simpkin," said the tailor, "where is my TWIST?"

But Simpkin hid a little parcel privately in the tea-pot, and spit and growled at the tailor; and if Simpkin had been able to talk, he would have asked: "Where is my MOUSE?"

"Alack, I am undone!" said the Tailor of Gloucester, and went sadly to bed.

All that night long Simpkin hunted and searched through the kitchen, peeping into cupboards and under the wainscot, and into the tea-pot where he had hidden that twist; but still he found never a mouse!

Whenever the tailor muttered and talked in his sleep, Simpkin said "Miaw-ger-r-w-s-s-ch!" and made strange horrid noises, as cats do at night.

For the poor old tailor was very ill with a fever, tossing and turning in his four-post bed; and still in his dreams he mumbled—"No more twist! No more twist!"

All that day he was ill, and the next day, and the next; and what should become of the cherry-coloured coat? In the tailor's shop in Westgate Street the embroidered silk and satin lay cut out upon the table—one-and-twenty button-holes—and who should come to sew them, when the window was barred, and the door was fast locked?

But that does not hinder the little brown mice; they run in and out without any keys through all the old houses in Gloucester!

Out of doors the market folks went trudging through the snow to buy their geese and turkeys, and to bake their Christmas pies; but there would be no Christmas dinner for Simpkin and the poor old Tailor of Gloucester.

The tailor lay ill for three days and nights; and then it was Christmas Eve, and very late at night. The moon climbed up over the roofs and chimneys, and looked down over the gateway into College Court. There were no lights in the windows, nor any sound in the houses; all the city of Gloucester was fast asleep under the snow.

And still Simpkin wanted his mice, and he mewed as he stood beside the four-post bed.

But it is in the old story that all the beasts can talk, in the night between Christmas Eve and Christmas Day in the morning (though there are very few folk that can hear them, or know what it is that they say).

When the Cathedral clock struck twelve there was an answer—like an echo of the chimes—and Simpkin heard it, and came out of the tailor's door, and wandered about in the snow.

From all the roofs and gables and old wooden houses in Gloucester came a thousand merry voices singing the old Christmas rhymes—all the old songs that ever I heard of, and some that I don't know, like Whittington's bells.

First and loudest the cocks cried out: "Dame, get up, and bake your pies!"

"Oh, dilly, dilly, dilly!" sighed Simpkin.

And now in a garret there were lights and sounds of dancing, and cats came from over the way.

"Hey, diddle, diddle, the cat and the fiddle! All the cats in Gloucester—except me," said Simpkin.

Under the wooden eaves the starlings and sparrows sang of Christmas pies; the jack-daws woke up in the Cathedral tower; and although it was the middle of the night the throstles and robins sang; the air was quite full of little twittering tunes.

But it was all rather provoking to poor hungry Simpkin!

Particularly he was vexed with some little shrill voices from behind a wooden lattice. I think that they were bats, because they always have very small voices—especially in a black frost, when they talk in their sleep, like the Tailor of Gloucester.

They said something mysterious that sounded like—

"Buz, quoth the blue fly; hum, quoth the bee;

Buz and hum they cry, and so do we!"

and Simpkin went away shaking his ears as if he had a bee in his bonnet.

From the tailor's shop in Westgate came a glow of light; and when Simpkin crept up to peep in at the window it was full of candles. There was a snippeting of scissors, and snappeting of thread; and little mouse voices sang loudly and gaily—

"Four-and-twenty tailors
Went to catch a snail,
The best man amongst them
Durst not touch her tail;
She put out her horns
Like a little kyloe cow,
Run, tailors, run! or she'll have you all e'en now!"

Then without a pause the little mouse voices went on again—

"Sieve my lady's oatmeal,
Grind my lady's flour,
Put it in a chestnut,
Let it stand an hour—"

"Mew! Mew!" interrupted Simpkin, and he scratched at the door.

But the key was under the tailor's pillow, he could not get in.

The little mice only laughed, and tried another tune—

"Three little mice sat down to spin,
Pussy passed by and she peeped in.
What are you at, my fine little men?
Making coats for gentlemen.
Shall I come in and cut off your threads?
Oh, no, Miss Pussy, you'd bite off our heads!"

"Mew! Mew!" cried Simpkin.
"Hey diddle dinketty?" answered the little mice—

"Hey diddle dinketty, poppetty pet!
The merchants of London they wear scarlet;
Silk in the collar, and gold in the hem,
So merrily march the merchantmen!"

They clicked their thimbles to mark the time, but none of the songs pleased Simpkin; he sniffed and mewed at the door of the shop.

"And then I bought
A pipkin and a popkin,
A slipkin and a slopkin,
All for one farthing—

—and upon the kitchen dresser!" added the rude little mice.

"Mew! scratch! scratch!" scuffled Simpkin on the window-sill; while the little mice inside sprang to their feet, and all began to shout at once in little twittering voices: "No more twist! No more twist!" And they barred up the window shutters and shut out Simpkin.

But still through the nicks in the shutters he could hear the click of thimbles, and little mouse voices singing—

"No more twist! No more twist!"

Simpkin came away from the shop and went home, considering in his mind. He found the poor old tailor without fever, sleeping peacefully.

Then Simpkin went on tip-toe and took a little parcel of silk out of the tea-pot, and looked at it in the moonlight; and he felt quite ashamed of his badness compared with those good little mice!

When the tailor awoke in the morning, the first thing which he saw upon the patchwork quilt, was a skein of cherry-coloured twisted silk, and beside his bed stood the repentant Simpkin!

"Alack, I am worn to a ravelling," said the Tailor of Gloucester, "but I have my twist!"

The sun was shining on the snow when the tailor got up and dressed, and came out into the street with Simpkin running before him.

The starlings whistled on the chimney stacks, and

the throstles and robins sang—but they sang their own little noises, not the words they had sung in the night.

"Alack," said the tailor, "I have my twist; but no more strength—nor time—than will serve to make me one single button-hole; for this is Christmas Day in the Morning! The Mayor of Gloucester shall be married by noon—and where is his cherry-coloured coat?"

He unlocked the door of the little shop in Westgate Street, and Simpkin ran in, like a cat that expects something.

But there was no one there! Not even one little brown mouse!

The boards were swept clean; the little ends of thread and the little silk snippets were all tidied away, and gone from off the floor.

But upon the table—oh joy! the tailor gave a shout—there, where he had left plain cuttings of silk—there lay the most beautifullest coat and embroidered satin waistcoat that ever were worn by a Mayor of Gloucester.

There were roses and pansies upon the facings of the coat; and the waistcoat was worked with poppies and corn-flowers.

Everything was finished except just one single cherry-coloured button-hole, and where that botton-hole was wanting there was pinned a scrap of paper with these words—in little teeny weeny writing—

NO MORE TWIST

And from then began the luck of the Tailor of Gloucester; he grew quite stout, and he grew quite rich.

He made the most wonderful waistcoats for all the rich merchants of Gloucester, and for all the fine gentlemen of the country round.

Never were seen such ruffles, or such embroidered cuffs and lappets! But his button-holes were the greatest triumph of it all.

The stitches of those button-holes were so neat—*so* neat—I wonder how they could be stitched by an old man in spectacles, with crooked old fingers, and a tailor's thimble.

The stitches of those button-holes were so small—*so* small—they looked as if they had been made by little mice!

CHRISTMAS CARDS

THE very first drawings that Beatrix Potter had published were six designs for Christmas cards, for which her pet rabbit, Benjamin Bunny, acted as a model. Throughout her life, Beatrix carried on giving home-made cards to her friends, sometimes in the form of simple hand-written notes, and she also painted pictures to be used on charity Christmas cards. Everyone loves a personal card, made just for them, and there are lots of basic ideas you can adapt to make different ones. Here are two easy designs to start off with, based on shapes cut out from card.

CHRISTMAS PUDDING CARD

You will need:
sheets of red, brown, green and black thin card (at least 20 cm [8"] square for the red card), or white card painted in these colors • scissors • a pencil • compasses, or a glass/cup about 10 cm (4") across and a glass/cup about 8-9 cm (3½") across, to draw round • glue • an envelope, at least 15 cm (6") high

How to make:

You can either cut your shapes straight out of the colored card, if you have it, or paint the card and then cut the shapes out when the paint is dry.

1 Fold in half a piece of red card (or white card painted red) at least 20 cm (8") square. Draw on it in pencil a circle at least 10 cm (4") across, so that the top of the circle comes above the fold. You can either draw round a glass of the right size or use compasses. There should be about 6 cm (2½") of fold at the top of this shape, which is the plate for the Christmas pudding. Cut round the edge of the circle and cut a tiny strip off the bottom to make a straight edge, so that the card stands up.

2 Now cut a circle out of brown card, or white card painted brown, with a diameter of about 8-9 cm (3½"). Stick this on to your plate so that the top half of the brown circle (which is your pudding) is above the fold, and the straight edge of the fold does not show.

3 Cut about 10 little oval shapes out of black card, or white card painted black. They can be very rough shapes, as they are meant to be raisins, which are not perfectly round. Stick them on to the pudding.

4 Cut three holly leaves out of green card, or white card painted green, and stick them on top of the pudding, with at least half of each leaf over the edge. Stick two or three tiny circles cut out of red card at the base of the leaves, for holly berries.

This is your basic Christmas pudding card. You can make it more elaborate by painting a design on the plate or adding glitter or white paint 'icing'. Write your message inside, and put the card in its envelope.

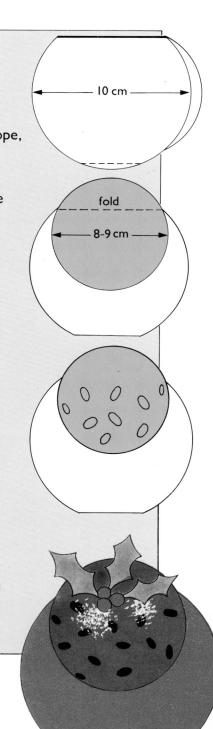

CHRISTMAS WREATH CARD

You will need:

red card • green card or green gummed paper (medium and dark green, if possible) • glue • a pencil • compasses, or a glass/cup about 11 cm (4½″) across and a small glass about 6 cm (2½″) across, to draw round • scissors • gold glitter, or sequins • an envelope, at least 15 cm (6″) high

How to make:

1 Fold in half a piece of red card about 24 cm (10″) square. Draw a circle in pencil at least 11 cm (4½″) across, so that the top of the circle comes above the fold (there should be a fold-line about 6 cm [2½″] long at the top of the circle). You can either draw round a glass of the right size, or use compasses. Cut out the circle.

2 Draw a smaller circle about 6 cm (2½″) across in the center of the larger one, and carefully cut this out to leave a ring shape. Cut a small strip off the bottom, so that the card stands up.

3 Now cut out your holly leaf shapes. You'll need about 30 in the medium green card or paper, and 10 in the dark green. The quickest way to cut them out is to fold the paper over and cut through 3 or 4 thicknesses, having drawn your leaves on in pencil first.

4 Stick the holly leaves on the red wreath so that they overlap. It looks nice if you can tuck the end of one leaf behind another, so that they appear woven together, but they can face in any direction.

5 Cut a few tiny circles out of the red card for holly berries and stick them on to the wreath. Dab on some patches of glue here and there, sprinkle on some glitter and lightly press it in with your finger, so that the card sparkles. Or you can stick on some sequins in the same way.

6 Write a circular message inside your card and keep it carefully in its envelope.

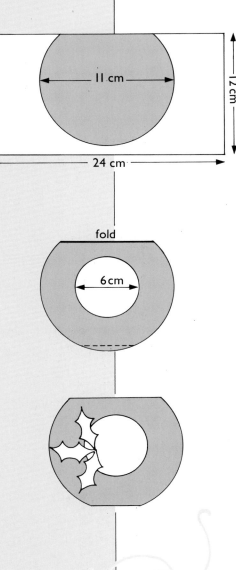

This is the basic idea for a Christmas holly wreath card. You can decorate the wreath in lots of different ways, adding a ribbon bow perhaps, or some tinsel among the leaves. Or you can make a shiny card by sticking on scraps of gold or silver doily and adding bells cut out of silver foil. Once you've started, the possibilities are endless!

A Picture Letter

SEE if you can make out what the youngest Flopsy Bunny is saying in his letter to Santa Claus.

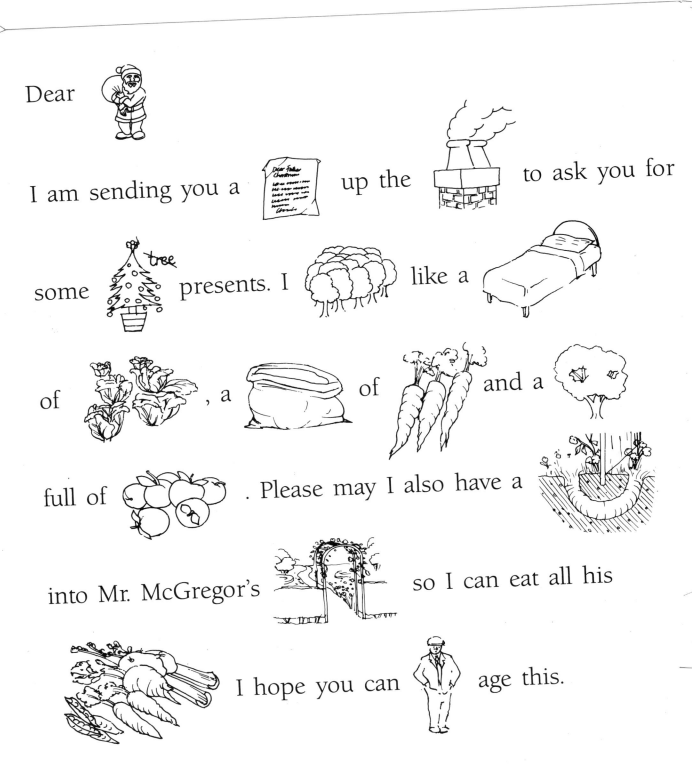

Dear [Santa],

I am sending you a [letter] up the [chimney] to ask you for some [tree] presents. I [would] like a [bed] of [lettuces], a [sack] of [carrots] and a [tree] full of [apples]. Please may I also have a [flowerbed] into Mr. McGregor's [gate] so I can eat all his [vegetables] I hope you can [man]age this.

Thank you,
Youngest Flopsy Bunny

LITTLE PIG ROBINSON
WORD SQUARE

LITTLE Pig Robinson has gone to Stymouth to do his Christmas shopping. Can you find the names of 21 things he buys in the word square below. They are written across, down, diagonally and backwards. The little pictures will give you some clues.

T	A	B	L	E	C	L	O	T	H	C	L	D
R	Y	L	L	O	H	N	A	I	H	S	E	A
E	Z	F	D	W	O	T	F	N	D	Y	M	T
E	A	F	S	B	C	A	X	S	B	O	O	E
O	G	N	B	D	O	T	O	E	F	T	N	S
D	L	I	R	H	L	Y	D	L	O	C	A	T
Y	R	A	Q	C	A	N	D	L	E	S	D	R
T	N	C	M	X	T	U	P	M	R	T	E	G
M	I	S	T	L	E	T	O	E	B	N	R	N
Z	P	A	T	L	F	S	K	D	W	E	A	I
B	E	L	L	S	K	C	L	Q	X	S	P	K
E	K	R	S	C	A	R	D	S	N	E	H	C
K	Q	D	O	R	A	N	G	E	S	R	T	O
A	Y	T	C	O	A	L	B	Z	F	P	D	T
C	C	A	P	U	D	D	I	N	G	C	A	S

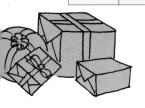

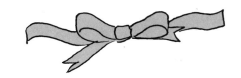

PRESENTS TO MAKE

MAKING presents adds to the fun as Christmas draws near. Here are some ideas for simple things to make for your family or friends.

CANDLE HOLDER

'Ninny Nanny Netticoat,
In a white petticoat,
  With a red nose, –
The longer she stands,
  The shorter she grows.'

From *Cecily Parsley's Nursery Rhymes*

You will need:
about half a pack of white modeling clay (from craft shops) or white, blue and brown modeling clay ● a candle ● old newspapers ● If using white modeling clay: white, blue and brown enamel paints ● a paintbrush ● white spirit or turpentine and an old yogurt pot, to clean the brush

How to make:

1 Take a piece of white modeling clay about the size of a small apple, roll it into a ball and press it down flat on the newspaper with the palm of your hand. You should aim to end up with a roughly circular, flat 'saucer' about 10 cm (4″) across.

2 Take another piece of white clay about half this size and roll it into a ball. Push the candle into the clay and mould the sides up around it, to make a little cup.

3 Take the candle out and place your cup in the middle of the saucer. Blend the bottom edges of the cup firmly into the saucer with your finger, so that the two are joined together. Try not to flatten the cup and place the candle in it again, to check it fits.

4 To make a rim for the saucer, roll out a long 'worm' from the

clay (blue clay, if using colors) with the palms of your hands, keeping it on the newspaper. It should be about 30 cm (12″) long. Press this down firmly on the edge of the saucer, to make a rim. If using colored clay, add another blue rim to the candle cup in the same way.

5 Now add your mouse. Take a small piece of clay (brown if using colors), roll it into a ball and pinch one end between your thumb and forefinger to make the head and nose of the mouse. Pinch out 2 ears, and make 2 eyes with the point of the pen. Stick your mouse firmly on the saucer beside the candle cup, then roll out another thin clay worm for the mouse's tail. Coil the tail round the candle cup, making sure it is firmly attached to the mouse! Smooth the join with your fingers.

6 Leave your candle holder a day or so to dry.

7 If using white modeling clay, paint the saucer white (including the base under the rim, but not the rim itself). Paint the outside of the candle cup white. Leave to dry, so that the paint doesn't run in the next stage, then paint the inside of the candle cup blue, and add a blue rim round the outer edge of cup. Paint the saucer rim blue, then paint the mouse and his tail brown.

PRESENTS TO MAKE

T HIS picture of two rabbits under an umbrella, one carrying a basket, was painted by Beatrix Potter to illustrate a booklet of poems called *A Happy Pair*. Packages and parcels in bright, jolly colors always look festive, and a basket is a useful and adaptable thing to make, because you can fill it with different little gifts to make a present for each member of your family.

PAPIER MÂCHÉ BASKETS

You will need:

2 or 3 old newspapers ● wallpaper paste, and an old container to mix it up in ● Vaseline ● an empty margarine container or ice-cream carton ● some medium-weight card ● scissors ● glue ● gold, red or green enamel paint ● a paintbrush ● white spirit or turpentine and an empty yogurt pot, to clean the brush ● some pretty ribbon or gold stick-on stars, to decorate

How to make:

The basket takes several days to make, as each stage needs time to dry.

1 First, spread out one of your newspapers on the table. Papier mâché is a messy business! Then tear another newspaper into thin strips, about 15 cm (6″) long.

2 Mix up about a quarter of the packet of wallpaper paste. Grease the outside of your margarine or ice-cream container with Vaseline.

3 Soak the newspaper strips in paste, and start applying them to the outside of your container, which acts as a mould for the basket. Build up layers along and across the basket, to make it strong, and squeeze any excess paste off the newspaper strips with your fingers. If the basket seems too wet, add more dry strips.

4 When you have applied a good many layers (you'll probably need a whole newspaper for each basket), put the basket in a warm place to dry out for a couple of days.

5 When the basket has dried out, ease it off the container and start to make the handle. Cut out 2 strips of card about 20 cm (8″) long, bend back tabs of about 2½ cm (1″) at each end, and glue the strips together, excluding the tabs. Curve the handle round, and when it has set, glue it to each side of the basket by the 4 tabs.

20 cm

2½cm

6 Stick some more newspaper strips over the joins of the handle, and neaten up the top edge of the basket by applying others to make a smooth finish. Leave the basket to dry out.

7 When the basket is dry, paint it with enamel paint (inside first, not forgetting the handle, then the outside, then, when this coat is dry, the bottom). Decorate with ribbon bows or gold stars.

PRESENTS TO EAT

'ON the fifth day the squirrels brought a present of wild honey; it was so sweet and sticky that they licked their fingers as they put it down upon the stone.'
From *The Tale of Squirrel Nutkin*

Everybody likes a treat at Christmas, and there are some delicious things that you can make to give as presents. Here are three ideas.

CHOCOLATE CHRISTMAS CRUNCH

You will need:

100 g (4 oz) wholemeal biscuits

50 g (2 oz) icing sugar or confectioner's sugar

125 g (5 oz) dark chocolate

100 g (4 oz) butter or margarine

some small sweets, such as Smarties or M and Ms

an empty egg carton

some silver foil, tissue or crepe paper

plus: a board, a rolling pin, a mixing bowl, a sieve, a small bowl, a saucepan, a wooden spoon and a shallow tin or earthenware dish, about 22 cm by 16 cm (8½″ by 6½″)

How to make:

1 Crush the biscuits, a few at a time, on the board with the rolling pin. Put all the crumbs in the mixing bowl, then sift the sugar into the mixing bowl and mix with the biscuit crumbs.

2 Break the chocolate into pieces and put in the small bowl with the butter or margarine.

3 Half fill the saucepan with hot water and stand the small bowl in it. Place saucepan and bowl on the stove, and turn the heat on low.

4 Stir the chocolate and butter/margarine mixture until it has melted, then pour over the biscuit crumbs in the mixing bowl and mix well with the wooden spoon.

5 Rub the tin or dish with a small amount of butter or margarine, then press the chocolate mixture into the tin and flatten it down with the wooden spoon.

6 Mark the mixture into squares while it is still in the tin, and press a small sweet into the top of each square.

7 Leave to set in the fridge for at least an hour, then carefully take the squares out of the tin (you may want some help with this).

8 Cut the top off an empty egg carton, fill each pocket with a little piece of crumpled-up silver foil, tissue or crepe paper, and place one or two chocolate squares in each one. Alternatively, you could give your sweets in a home-made basket (see previous page), or a pretty tin.

SUGAR MICE

You will need:

225 g (8 oz) ready-made fondant icing (cake decoration)

pink food coloring

tiny silver balls or chocolate drops, for eyes

plus: a knife and an airtight container.

How to make:

1 Cut the icing in half, and knead a few drops of pink food coloring into one half until the paste is smooth (catch the drops in the lid of the bottle, to avoid spilling the coloring). Half your mice can be pink, and half white.

2 Pinch off pieces of icing and roll into balls,

larger ones for the bodies, smaller for the heads. Press the heads on to the bodies, moulding them together around the neck.

3 Roll out thin sausages of paste with your fingers for the tails, and press them on to the mice's bodies. Press in chocolate drops or silver balls for eyes, or add tiny pieces of paste in the contrasting color (pink for white mice, white for pink ones).

4 Store the mice in a cool place, in an airtight container, until ready to be given.

BREAD-AND-BUTTER PICKLES

You will need:

2 large cucumbers

350 g (¾ lb) onions

50 g (2 oz) salt

350 ml (12 fl oz) cider vinegar

350 g (12 oz) sugar

2 tablespoons mustard seed

2 teaspoons celery seed

¼ teaspoon turmeric

¼ teaspoon cayenne pepper

some sticky labels for the jars

plus: a knife, a chopping board, a bowl, a colander, a large saucepan, a ladle or large spoon, about 3 or 4 glass jars, with lids (old coffee jars are ideal, as plastic lids are better than metal ones)

Don't forget *to ask a grown-up for permission before you use a knife or heat the oven or burners.*

How to make:

1 First of all, sterilize the jars by heating them in a moderate oven (without their lids) for about 20 minutes.

2 Cut the cucumbers into 5 mm (¼ inch), thickish slices. Slice the onions as finely as you can.

3 Mix the onions, salt and cucumber together in a large bowl. Leave to stand for three hours, then drain and rinse them in the colander under a cold tap.

4 Bring all the other ingredients to the boil in a large pan, then add the cucumber and onions. Lower the heat and simmer for 2 minutes (don't let the mixture bubble too fiercely, or the pickles will be limp).

5 You may want some help with this part. Carefully ladle the cucumbers into the hot, sterilized jars and cover with the vinegar and onion mixture. Seal the jars.

6 Write a jolly label for the jar, including the date, decorating it with felt pens if you like.

PRESENTS TO MAKE

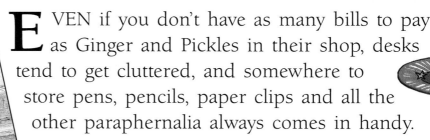

E VEN if you don't have as many bills to pay as Ginger and Pickles in their shop, desks tend to get cluttered, and somewhere to store pens, pencils, paper clips and all the other paraphernalia always comes in handy.

DESK-TIDY

You will need:

3 white paper plates, about 18 cm (7″) across ● glue ● a pencil ● scissors ● I metre (I yard) of sticky-backed plastic in a plain, bright color (a plain color is easier for patching awkward places) ● about 3 or 4 inner cardboard tubes (from toilet rolls, kitchen paper rolls, etc)

How to make:

1 Stick together your paper plates one on top of the other with glue to make a firm base.

2 Draw round the plates with a pencil on the paper backing of the plastic. Draw a border about 5 cm (2″) larger than this and cut round it. Peel away the paper backing and place the plastic over your plates, smoothing out any air bubbles, then turn the plates over. Cut the border down to the plates at roughly 2½ cm (1″) intervals, and stick over the rim of the plates, overlapping the cut edges.

Bottom of plates

Plastic

3 Next, cover your tubes with plastic too. If possible, they should be of different lengths — perhaps 2 toilet rolls, plus I cut in half to make 2 small containers, and a taller inner tube from some kitchen paper. Cut out a piece of plastic wide enough to go right round each tube, and with at least 5 cm (2″) extra to overlap each end. Peel off the backing and wrap the plastic carefully round the tube, smoothing out air bubbles as you go. Cut the plastic down to the tube at 2½ cm (1″) intervals and stick over the rim of the tube, as before. If there are any wrinkles or gaps, cut out a patch from some spare plastic and stick it over the bodgy area.

4 When you have covered all the tubes, decide how you want them to be grouped and stick the tallest one down first. To do this, cut out 2 strips of plastic, about 5 cm (2″) long and 2½ cm (1″) wide, peel away the backing and stick each strip to opposite *inside* edges of the covered tube. Overlap them in the middle to form a sticky 'bridge', and press your tube down on to the plate.

5 Stick down the next tube in the same way, and attach it to the first tube with another strip of sticky plastic, about 5 cm (2″) wide and as long as the shorter tube. Fold this strip in half lengthwise with the backing outwards, remove the backing and carefully position the folded edge where the tubes touch, sticking them together.

6 Stick all the tubes to the plate and to each other. You can make the base join extra strong by cutting out a strip of plastic about 2½ cm (1″) wide, making slits along the edge and sticking it over the join as shown in the diagram.

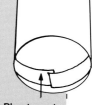

Plastic strips

Plastic strip, sticky side out, stick here

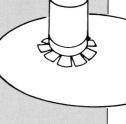

H ERE is Ribby putting her pie made of mouse into the oven. She would have needed a cloth or glove to take the pie out again when it was cooked, and an oven glove is an easy present to make. Choose brightly colored felt, or make it in black felt to use as a coal glove for laying an open fire.

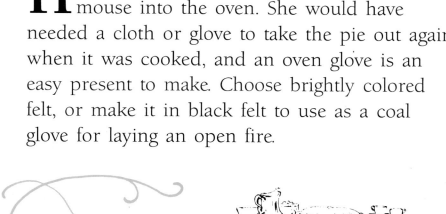

AN OVEN GLOVE OR COAL GLOVE

You will need:

a sheet of paper ● pencil ● 3 large pieces of felt, about 30 cm (12'') square ● scissors ● pins ● a needle ● embroidery thread ● some felt scraps, in contrasting colors ● glue ● a short length of seam binding or ribbon

How to make:

1 Ask an adult to lay his or hand flat down on the sheet of paper, and draw round it in pencil, leaving a border of at least 2½ cm (1'') all the way round. Draw a wide cuff at the wrist. The whole hand needs to fit through this opening, so it should measure at least 15 cm (6'').

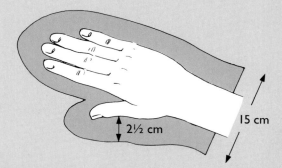

2½ cm

15 cm

2 Cut this pattern out, pin it on the 3 thicknesses of felt and cut around it.
3 Sew around the outside of the glove with the embroidery thread, using blanket stitch or simple overstitching, and making sure you catch all 3 thicknesses of felt.

Blanket Stitch   Oversewing

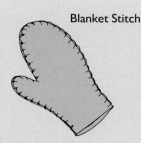   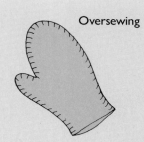

4 You need to have the double thickness of felt on the inner (palm) side of the glove, so when you reach the wrist opening, hold the glove with the thumb pointing to the left, and sew the bottom 2 layers of felt to each other with blanket stitch. (If you are giving the glove to a left-handed person, the glove should face the other way, with the thumb pointing to the right.) Then hem round the upper edge of the opening in blanket stitch, to match.
5 Decorate the upper surface of the glove with your felt scraps, sticking on the shapes or oversewing them on. You could choose a cat, some fruit, or some bright flowers perhaps. If you stick the shapes on, adding some embroidery detail (the cat's eyes or whiskers, for example) will make them extra secure.
6 Lastly, sew on a ribbon or seam-binding loop at the top inside corner of the glove, so that it can be hung up.

Blanket Stitch   Overstitch

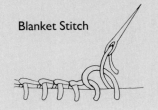   

JOIN-THE-DOTS PICTURE

JOIN the dots to complete this picture of Hunca Munca and Tom Thumb putting a sixpence into one of Jane and Lucinda's stockings. After you've finished, why not color in the picture? You can find the finished painting on page 57 of *The Tale of Two Bad Mice.*

JUMBLED CARDS PUZZLE

PETER Rabbit is out delivering Christmas cards, but he is having a lot of trouble reading the jumbled-up names on the envelopes. Can you work out which animal or person each card is addressed to? (Their names all appear somewhere in this book.) After you've done the puzzle, you can check your answers on the last page, and then color in the picture.

1 FLYSPO NYNUB

2 RM MEEYRJ RHSEFI

3 SRM UTELTEISMTO

4 IETTLL GPI BROONSIN

5 RLAOTI FO COELSETGRU

6 RPTEE BTAIRB

CHRISTMAS TABLE DECORATIONS

There's nothing like a really festive-looking table to add to the fun of a Christmas lunch or tea party. A color scheme, like red, green and gold or pink, grey and silver, will add to the effect if it is repeated in the tablecloth, napkins, centerpiece and placecards.

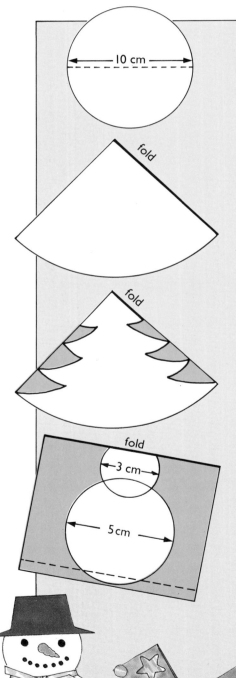

CHRISTMAS TREE PLACECARDS

You will need:
some thin colored card ● a pencil ● scissors ● a felt-tip pen (a gold marker pen is especially effective) ● some stick-on stars, glitter and glue, to decorate

How to make:
Draw a circle in pencil about 10 cm (4″) across on the card, using compasses or a cup to draw round, and cut this out. Fold the circle in half and cut it down the middle, to make 2 semicircles. Fold each semicircle in half again and draw little triangles at each side, for your Christmas tree shape (see diagram). Cut these triangles out, making sure that the 2 quarters of the shape remain joined by the fold at the top. Stand them up on the round edges and you have a little rocking tree. Write the person's name at the bottom in felt pen, and decorate with stars and blobs of glue sprinkled with glitter.

SNOWMAN PLACECARDS

You will need:
thin white card ● some scraps of dark-colored and red card. card ● scissors ● glue ● felt-tip pens in black, red and gold (if possible) ● scraps of thin ribbon.

How to make:
Fold your white card in half and draw 2 inter-connecting circles on it, a smaller one about 3 cm (1¼″) across on top of a larger one about 5 cm (2″) across. At least 2½ cm (1″) of the smaller circle should be over the fold. Cut your snowman shape out and cut a strip off the bottom circle, so he stands flat. Stick on a hat cut out of the darker card, and tie a scrap of thin ribbon round his neck as a scarf. Cut out a square of red card, write the person's name on it in gold or black, and stick it on the snowman's tummy. Draw the snowman's eyes and mouth in black, with a red carrot nose, and draw in some arms to hold the namecard.

A CANDLE CENTERPIECE

You will need:

a cardboard tube (from a toilet roll or kitchen paper roll)
● some thick white paper or thin card ● pretty wrapping paper
● scissors ● glue ● a paper plate about 15 cm (6″) across
● a scrap of thick card ● a gold felt-tip or gold paint
● a knife ● glitter and ribbon to decorate

glue

How to make:

First of all, draw round the bottom of your cardboard tube on the white paper or card, add a border of about 2½ cm (1″) all the way round, and cut round this larger circle. Cut the border down to the inner circle at roughly 1 cm (½″) intervals, and spread glue over these tabs. Position the tube on this inner circle and stick the tabs down on to the sides of the tube, so covering the open end. Repeat this process at the other end of the tube. Then, do exactly the same with a piece of wrapping paper, spreading glue right over the tabs and inner circle, and sticking it to the white paper or card at one end of your tube. Next, cut a rectangle of wrapping paper the same height as your tube and long enough to wrap round it. Stick this over the tube, covering the tabs at each end. Cover your paper plate by drawing round it in pencil on the back of the wrapping paper, adding a border of about 5 cm (2″) all round, cutting the larger circle out and cutting tabs, once again. Spread glue over the top of the plate, stick the wrapping paper circle over it, turn it over and stick the tabs down to the bottom of the plate. Then fix your candle in the center of its holder by spreading glue on the end covered only in white card and sticking it in place. Lastly, draw a flame shape on the thick card, cut this out and color it gold on both sides with felt-tip pen or paint. Add some glue and glitter, and fix the flame into a slot at the top of the candle, about 2 cm (¾″) long, which you have carefully cut with the point of a sharp knife. You may need help with this. Tie some ribbon round the bottom of the candle to make it look even jollier, or you can heap the plate with gold or silver baubles for extra effect.

Wrapping paper

A Christmas Tea Party

Why not ask some friends round to a Christmas tea party? You can decorate the table using some of the ideas on the previous pages. Add a paper tablecloth, napkins and cups, perhaps, plus lots of festive food. Here are some recipes.

CHRISTMAS-TREE TOASTIES

You will need:
brown or white sliced bread
(1 slice makes 1 toasty)

butter or margarine

tomato ketchup

enough grated cheddar cheese to cover the number of slices you are making

tiny pieces of raw red or green pepper or carrot

a stick of raw carrot for the tree trunk

plus: a table knife, a grill pan and a large plate, to put the toasties on while they cool

How to make:

1 Cut each slice of bread into quarters, arrange them on the grill pan, and toast *on one side only* under the grill.

2 Spread the untoasted side of each quarter with butter or margarine, then a thin layer of tomato ketchup, and lastly, top with grated cheese.

3 Grill the quarters lightly until the cheese melts. While the cheese is still hot, overlap the quarters to make a Christmas-tree shape, pressing the point of each triangle into the melted cheese of the one above. When the cheese has cooled, the toasties will be held in this shape, though you'll need to handle them carefully.

4 Before the cheese has cooled completely, decorate the trees with tiny pieces of raw carrot or pepper, and add a stick of raw carrot for the tree trunk.

5 Place the toasties on a large plate to finish cooling.

CHEESY BISCUITS

You will need:
175 g (6 oz) plain flour
1 teaspoon of salt
75 g (3 oz) fine semolina
110 g (4 oz) grated cheddar cheese
175 g (6 oz) butter or margarine
a tube of cream cheese, to decorate

plus: a large mixing bowl, a baking sheet or tray, a table knife, a rolling pin and a board, decorative biscuit cutters (Christmas trees, stars or moons, if you have them) and a wire cooling tray.

How to make:

1 Heat the oven to Gas Mark 2 (300 F) and grease the baking sheet with a little butter or margarine.

2 Mix together the flour, salt and semolina in a bowl, then add the grated cheese and butter or margarine, cut into pieces with a table knife. Mix them all together with your fingers until you have a smooth dough.

3 Dust the rolling pin and the board with flour and roll out the dough until it is about ½ cm (¼") thick. Stamp out shapes with the cutters, arrange them on the baking sheet and bake in the middle of the oven for 1 hour.

4 Cool the biscuits on a wire rack, then pipe round the edges with cream cheese.

CARROT AND CUCUMBER CRACKERS

You will need:
a cucumber
225 g (8 oz) carrots
plus: a vegetable peeler, a chopping board
and a sharp knife

How to make:

1 Wash the cucumber and peel the
carrots. Cut the carrots and cucumber into
vertical sections about 8 cm
(3″) long on the chopping
board, and then cut them very
carefully *lengthwise* into flat
strips, about ½ cm (¼″) thick.
Cut the cucumber strips in
half, lengthwise.

2 Trim these strips into
cracker shapes with your knife,
and pile them into a pretty
bowl.

FROSTY CHRISTMAS PUDDING

You will need:
1 litre (2 pt) chocolate ice cream
100 g (4 oz) dried apricots
100 g (4 oz) dark chocolate drops
225 g (8 oz) raisins
small carton of double or whipping cream
some sprigs of real or artificial holly, to
decorate
plus: a sharp knife, a chopping board, a 1½
litre (3 pt) pudding basin, a freezer, a
wooden spoon, a larger bowl or saucepan, a
serving plate, a wire whisk and a small bowl
to whip the cream

How to make:

1 Chop the dried apricots into little pieces
on the chopping board.

2 Turn the ice cream out into the larger
bowl and beat it gently with the wooden
spoon until it softens. Stir in the apricots,
chocolate drops and raisins and pack into
the 1½ litre (3 pt) pudding basin. Freeze
until firm.

3 Fill the larger bowl or saucepan with
boiling water and carefully dip the pudding
basin in for a few seconds, to loosen the ice
cream (ask an adult to help
you with this). Turn the
pudding out on to a serving
plate and place back in the
freezer until ready to serve.

4 When ready to serve,
whip the cream with the
whisk in a small bowl until
thick but not stiff, pour over
the pudding and stick in your
holly.

WRAPPING UP

Beatrix Potter was very interested in printing; not just the printing of her Peter Rabbit books, but decorative printing on to fabric or paper. Her grandfather, Edmund Potter, owned a huge factory which produced designs on calico and Beatrix even arranged for some of her books to be specially bound using Edmund Potter & Co. fabric.

You can create some exclusive hand-printed paper at home, for wrapping up Christmas presents. Matching gift tags are easy too.

You will need:
2 or 3 medium-sized potatoes
a small knife (not too sharp)
red and green poster paints, or special 'printing colors' (from an art shop)
sheets of colored tissue or crepe paper, or silver foil, for printing on
a paintbrush
old newspapers

How to make:

1 Cut a potato in half and then lightly score your image on the cut surface with a knife. You could choose a Christmas tree, a bell or a star – something fairly simple and easy to cut out.

2 Carefully cut away a thin layer of potato from around the image so that it stands out. Make the edges as neat as possible (you may want some help with this.)

3 Paint the image with red or green paint, keeping everything on the old newspaper, and then press the image firmly on to your paper or foil (it's easiest to print on the dull side of the foil). Hold the paper flat with one hand so that your printed image

doesn't smudge and lift the potato cleanly off. If part of the design doesn't come out, don't worry – you can always touch it up with the paintbrush.

4 Repeat the process, repainting your potato printer when necessary, so that the paper has rows, or clusters, of stars or Christmas trees, or whatever you are printing. Leave room for a second image, though.

5 Cut another potato half in the same way, choosing a different design, and paint it with the contrasting color. Complete your wrapping paper by printing on this second image, and leave it to dry.

GIFT TAGS

You will need:

materials for printing listed on opposite page

thin card, in red or green

scissors

gift-wrapping ribbon (gold looks nice)

glitter

glue

a hole puncher, if you have one

How to make:

1 Fold over about 5 cm (2″) of the card down a long edge and cut off this double layer to make one long, thin, folded card. Cut this into 5 cm (2″) sections to make several tiny cards.

2 Print each card with a single image from your wrapping paper printing using a color of paint which contrasts with the card. Add spots of glue and some glitter to make your tags sparkle.

3 Punch a hole through both layers of the top-left-hand corner of the gift tag, or ask an adult to make a hole with the point of some scissors or a knife, if you don't have a hole punch.

4 Cut off about 20 cm (8″) of ribbon and cut it into 4 narrow lengths. Thread one length through each hole, knot it and trim off the excess.

5 Write your message inside the tag, then tie it to your parcel or stick it on with a small piece of sellotape.

Wishing You A Merry Christmas

CHRISTMAS TREE DECORATIONS

THERE are lots of Christmas tree decorations to buy, but it's fun to make your own, and you can start fairly early in the Christmas season. One thing to remember is that the ornaments ought to look pretty on both sides.

POPCORN AND CRANBERRY STRINGS

You will need:
some un-popped or ready-made popcorn (the uncoated variety) ● some fresh cranberries ● a needle threaded with about 45 cm (18") strong cotton

How to make:
If using un-popped corn, cook it up according to the instructions on the packet. Tie a knot at the end of the thread and string on the berries and corn alternately. When your corn and berry string reaches about 30 cm (12"), tie another knot at the end and cut off the remaining cotton. Simply loop the string over a branch of your Christmas tree for a lovely glowing decoration.

SNOWFLAKES AND 'STAINED-GLASS WINDOWS'

You will need:
a piece of medium-weight card ● some metallic sticky tape ● 2 silver or gold paper doilies ● glue ● scissors ● a knife ● some ribbon for hanging the ornament

How to make:
Cut out a snowflake or other design from one doily, then cover both sides of the card with shiny sticky tape until you have an area large enough to stick your doily design on to. Cut around the design, turn the card over, and stick a matching doily shape on to the other side. Carefully make a hole at the top with the point of your knife, thread through some ribbon to make a hanging loop, knot it and tie a bow at the top.

MINI STOCKINGS

You will need:
a piece of felt about 22 cm (8½") square ● scissors ● pins ● a needle ● some embroidery thread in a contrasting color ● some pretty ribbon ● fabric glue ● stick-on paper stars or sequins ● kitchen or tissue paper, for padding

How to make:
Fold your felt square in half, then draw a stocking shape on a rough piece of paper that will fit your felt rectangle. Cut this pattern out, pin it on the double thickness of felt and cut round it. Unpin the pattern, pin the two stocking pieces together and sew the outside edges together in blanket stitch, except for the top edges. Stick on stripes cut from your ribbon, and stars or sequins too. The paper stars will not stick to the felt quite so well, but you can dab on some glue to make the join stronger. Stick or sew a loop of ribbon at a top inside corner of the stocking to hang it up, and lightly pad the inside with torn-up kitchen paper or tissue paper.

THE ANIMALS' CHRISTMAS

BETWEEN the stream and the tree where the hens were
roosting, there was a white untrodden slope. Only one
tree grew there, a very small spruce, a little Christmas tree
some four foot high. As the night grew darker — the branches
of this little tree became all tipped with light, and wreathed
with icicles and chains of frost. Brighter and brighter it shone,
until it seemed to bear a hundred fairy lights; not like the
yellow gleam of candles, but a clear white incandescent light.

Small voices and music began to mingle with the sound of
the water. Up by the snowy banks, from the wood and from
the meadow beyond, tripped scores of little shadowy creatures,
advancing from the darkness into the light. They trod a circle
on the snow around the Christmas tree, dancing gaily hand-in-
hand. Rabbits, moles, squirrels, and wood-mice — even the half
blind mole, old Samson Velvet, danced hand-in-paw with a
wood-mouse and a shrew — whilst a hedgehog played the bag-
pipes beneath the fairy spruce.

from *The Fairy Caravan*

ANSWERS TO PUZZLES

A Picture Letter
Dear Santa Claus, I am sending you a *letter* up the *chimney* to ask you for some *Christmas* presents. I *would* like a *bed* of *lettuces*, a *sack* of *carrots* and a *tree* full of *apples*. Please may I also have a *tunnel* into Mr. McGregor's *garden* so I can eat all his *vegetables*? I hope you can *manage* this.

Little Pig Robinson Word Square
tablecloth, tree, holly, tinsel, toys, lemonade, dates, ribbon, chocolate, candles, nuts, presents, stockings, mistletoe, bells, cards, cake, crackers, coal, pudding, oranges

Jumbled Cards Puzzle
1, Flopsy Bunny; 2, Mr. Jeremy Fisher; 3, Mrs. Tittlemouse; 4, Little Pig Robinson; 5, Tailor of Gloucester; 6, Peter Rabbit

FREDERICK WARNE
Published by the Penguin Group
27 Wrights Lane, London W8 5TZ, England
Penguin Books USA Inc., 375 Hudson Street, New York, New York 10014, USA
Penguin Books Australia Ltd, Ringwood, Victoria, Australia
Penguin Books Canada Ltd, 2801 John Street, Markham, Ontario, Canada L3R 1B4
Penguin Books (NZ) Ltd, 182-190 Wairau Road, Auckland 10, New Zealand

Penguin Books Ltd, Registered Offices: Harmondsworth, Middlesex, England

First published 1990
3 5 7 9 10 8 6 4

Text by Jennie Walters
Design and illustrations by The Pinpoint Design Company
Advent calendar devised and illustrated by Alex Vining

ISBN 0 7232 3778 6

Printed and bound in Great Britain by
William Clowes Limited,
Beccles and London